THE
GREAT GREEN
FOREST

Paul Geraghty

RED FOX

High up in the great green forest, the sun began to rise.

Way down in the deep dark shadows, a treemouse
was curling up to sleep.

Creech! Creech! Woop! Woop! chirped the
frogs. The sounds were screechy, the
sounds were sharp: *Woopoo! Woopoo!
Creech! Creech!*

'Stop that noise!' yelled the treemouse, 'I'm trying to sleep!'

But all she heard was the *Zee-zee-zee-zee!* of a cicada somewhere outside. *Zee-zee-zee-zee!* Then the *Hmmm* of a humming bird, *Hmmm* over here and *Hmmm* over there.

'Stop that noise!' yelled the treemouse, 'I'm trying to sleep!'

Then *Keeoo...kedik-kedik-kedik!* came the calls from the forest crown. Toucans pierced the curtain of green with a *Keeoo...kedik-kedik-kedik!*

'Stop that noise!' yelled the treemouse, 'I'm trying to sleep!' But the forest was alive with songs and sounds.

Yaag! Screecha-screecha-screecha! squawked a macaw, *Yaag! SCRAAA! SCRAAA!* squawked another.

'Stop that noise!' yelled the treemouse, 'I'm trying to sleep!'

But her voice was drowned by the monkeys that bickered in the branches. *Duwoop! Ooo-ooo-ooo-ooo!* whooped one, *Yeek! Yeek!* screamed the others.

'Stop that noise!' yelled the treemouse, 'I'm trying to sleep!' And suddenly the forest fell silent. All she heard was the echo of her own voice.

Animals clung in silence, not daring to move or make a sound.

Even the cats that ruled the forest now cowered in the quiet. That's better! thought the treemouse.

But it wasn't. She couldn't sleep.
The silence grew worse than any
noise, until finally she cried out,
'Please make some noise! I'm
trying to sleep!'

She waited. And then there was a noise. She heard a distant *Brrrm, brrrm . . .* and then a *C-r-r-r-r-r-RACKA-DACKA-RACKA* **SHOONG!** that shook her to the ground.

A tree had fallen. And a gaping hole was left in the crown of the great green forest.

C-r-r-r-r-r-RACKA-DACKA-RACKA
SHOONG!
Another tree came down!

Brrrm, BRRRM . . . an ugly sound made the ground shudder. And the treemouse knew her tree would be next.

She looked up at her home; then she turned to the terrible sound. And at the top of her voice she yelled, 'STOP THAT NOISE!'

But that noise didn't stop.
Brrrm, it drew closer, *BRRRM,* till the earth
thundered; *BRRRM!* it grew louder, **BRRRM!**
till the earth shook. But the treemouse stood
firm.

Then something made the driver stop. And when he stopped, he felt the silence. He saw the broken trees. He saw the fallen nests.

And he sensed angry eyes watching him.

So he sat and he thought. He stayed there and thought till the sun went down. And when it was dark, he went away.

And he never came back.

Now way up in the great green forest, the trees are growing again.

And deep down in the dark shadows, a treemouse
curls up and closes her eyes. She listens to the songs
and sounds of the forest, which tell her that, for now,
she can sleep in peace.

For
Extremely Tiny Most Miniature
and extremely tiny people everywhere

THE GREAT GREEN FOREST
A RED FOX BOOK 0 09 187723 7

First published in Great Britain by Hutchinson Children's Books
an imprint of Random House Children's Books

Hutchinson edition published 1992
Red Fox edition published 1994

1 3 5 7 9 10 8 6 4 2

Red Fox Books are published by Random House Children's Books,
61–63 Uxbridge Road, London W5 5SA,
a division of The Random House Group Ltd,
in Australia by Random House Australia (Pty) Ltd,
20 Alfred Street, Milsons Point, Sydney, NSW 2061, Australia,
in New Zealand by Random House New Zealand Ltd,
18 Poland Road, Glenfield, Auckland 10, New Zealand,
and in South Africa by Random House (Pty) Ltd,
Endulini, 5A Jubilee Road, Parktown 2193, South Africa

THE RANDOM HOUSE GROUP Limited Reg. No. 954009

www.**kids**at**r**andomhouse.co.uk
www.paulgeraghty.net

A CIP catalogue record for this book is available from the British Library.

Printed in Hong Kong